The Enclave

The Enclave

Anne Charnock

NewCon Press
England

First published in the UK by NewCon Press
41 Wheatsheaf Road, Alconbury Weston, Cambs, PE28 4LF
February 2017

NCP 113 (limited edition hardback)
NCP 114 (softback)

10 9 8 7 6 5 4 3 2 1

ISBN:

978-1-910935-33-0 (hardback)
978-1-910935-34-7 (softback)

Cover art by Chris Moore
Cover layout by Andy Bigwood

Minor editorial meddling by Ian Whates
Book layout by Storm Constantine

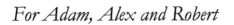

For Adam, Alex and Robert

One

At the rooftop sink, with the sun already burning my back, I turn on the cold tap, lean over and rinse my itchy scalp and scarecrow hair. Cold water never runs from the cold tap – well, not since summer started, not even in the morning after the storage tank has cooled during the night. The tank bakes all day in the sunshine and by the evening the cold tap always runs hot.

Just because the tap is labelled *C*, doesn't mean it is *C*.

Ma Lexie calls out: "Caleb, over here. Now."

She leads me across the flat roof of our housing block, past the solar arrays, towards a wooden hut – the living quarters of Mr. Ben, the overseer. I walk as close as I can behind her because she smells like fresh oranges. She looks as light as a feather; she could float away in the breeze. Her thin sleeveless dress is printed with wild flowers and owls. As the fabric ripples, the owls with stretched out wings seem to fly. I'm wearing only my shorts, and I'm barefoot. My hair drips onto my shoulders and down my back, bringing a memory of being tickled.

Ma Lexie swipes the air above her head with her right hand. I glance across to the roof of the next housing block; is she waving to Odette? No, she can't be. Odette is facing away from us, reaching up with both hands. Squinting, I see she's cutting dead flowers from a climbing rose. I worry about the thorns; don't prick yourself, Odette.

Ma Lexie is now swiping back and forth as though smacking a tall person across the face, first with the back of her hand and then her open palm.

"Don't panic, Ma Lexie," I say. An early-rising honey bee is harassing her. But I reckon the bee is still sleepy, like me.

We're on the bee's flight path from the hives, two roofs away, to the lavender farms west of the enclave. When I first arrived here five months ago, Ma Lexie told me I'd get used to the bees. They'd continue on their way if I didn't make a fuss. She's making a fuss herself and mutters the usual complaints – "Shouldn't be allowed," and then, "Affecting my business."

"The enclave council should ban the hives, Ma Lexie, shouldn't they?" I'm trying to nudge her towards a better mood, because I reckon I'm heading straight for trouble. In her left hand, she grips the candy-striped shirt that I worked on yesterday. Mr. Ben was disgusted with how I'd sewn the shirt's collar. He yanked my ear, hard. Called me a frikkin' idiot and told me to stop work on the shirt. He shouted – said he'd shift me back to baby work, unpicking seams, sewing on buttons, if I couldn't think of anything sensible to make. I guess he complained to the boss, Ma Lexie, about me.

Anyway, what does *he* know? After the yanking, he walked off, and I watched his fleshy rounded back as he grumped away across the roof to his hut. I snuck to the back of our workshed and pushed the shirt under my bedding roll. I'd already unpicked the collar, and in its place I'd started sewing a strip of dark mock fur; it made the shirt look mean, kinda dangerous. A brilliant remake, and I thought Ma Lexie would agree. I carried on with the half-finished job during our evening play time. Zach and Mikey wanted me to join the button-flicking game that I'd invented, but I told them to practise without me.

Ma Lexie grips my shoulder as we stand outside Mr. Ben's hut. She shakes the shirt at me. I feel hurt; while I was washing at the sink, Ma Lexie had dug around in my things. She says, "Mr. Ben came to see me yesterday. Not happy about your work, told me about this!"

I jump in fast. "Mr. Ben knows shit. I'm finishing the shirt in my own time, Ma Lexie. It's going to look brilliant when it's nicely pressed." I'd planned to finish sewing the fur collar and sneak it into the pile for pressing. Honest, I thought Ma Lexie would like it; I thought she'd smile.

"Mr. Ben wants me to throw you out. Send you to work at the family premises."

I stare at her. We're both wide-eyed. The family premises, as she calls it, is the centre of the family's rubbish and recycling business. I've never been there. I've been off the roof for less than twenty minutes a week.

She throws the hut's door wide open and steps inside. I grab it as it swings back and keep it steady in the warm breeze.

"This is yours now, Caleb."

I step inside for the first time. It stinks of Mr. Ben. Sweat and chlorine. My empty stomach tightens.

"Where...?" I look around expecting him to leap out and clout me one.

"I've decided Mr. Ben isn't cut out for the fashion business. No imagination."

"But where...?"

"He's better suited to the dirty side of the operation, don't you think?" She frowns at me. "You won't be seeing him anytime soon. So, clean this place out. Look after it better than he did. You're the overseer now."

I look down at the shirt, and she hands it over.

"Any of this fur left?" she asks. I nod. "Then, make as many as you can. I think they'll sell."

She's dead right. "I need better quality shirts than this, Ma Lexie. I want them to look... *sharp*. Tailored office shirts, that sort of thing. They'll look like a uniform, for a team or a gang."

She raises an eyebrow, hesitating. Does she think I'm being dumb?

She says, "Finish this one today and I'll try it out tomorrow at the market stall. And from now on, you'll be doing the weekend markets with me."

The markets! I want to hug her, but I've never seen anyone touch Ma Lexie. It's like she's too perfect, like the touch would burn you. And I don't know why we call her Ma – bet she's only thirty. I kneel down and kiss the hem of her dress.

"Up," she says.

"The shirt will be amazing, Ma Lexie."

She digs into a pocket in her dress and holds out two keys on a greasy black ribbon, which I've only ever seen hanging around Mr. Ben's neck, the keys always nestled in his thick mat of chest hair. One key is for the padlock for Mr. Ben's hut. *My* hut. The other is for the steel door – the roof access to the building's internal stairs.

"Your new job starts in five minutes," she says. "Come down to my flat and collect the kids' breakfasts."

As I reach out for the keys, she pulls back, and I freeze. It's a hoax. She'll laugh and Mr. Ben will leap out and whack me. She says, slowly and gently, "No second chance, Caleb. Don't let me catch you going downstairs and wandering off. You know I'd find you. Everyone knows Ma Lexie." I take the keys. Before she releases her grip, she says, "When everyone sees you at the market with me, they will know exactly who you are. That you're my new boy. Everyone will memorise your face. Understand?" And with that she heads back across the roof and retreats down the stairs to her top-floor flat. Yes, I can trust her – what you see is what you get with Ma Lexie.

I'm Ma Lexie's new boy. I like the sound of that. Better than *the kid dumped on the road*, but no one knows about that around here. It's a new start.

I can't do much in five minutes to clear Mr. Ben's mess, but

I drag out the mattress and prop it against the side of the hut. If the mattress soaks up the sun, it's likely to *air out*, as my mother would say. I've no idea what airing out means. Does a smell dry out? Won't the bed bugs thrive in the heat? Or does bright light kill them off? Anyway, until I'm rid of the stench, I'll continue to sleep with the sky as my blanket.

I wedge open the door by leaning Mr. Ben's wooden chair – *my* wooden chair – against the door's crossbeam. I step inside and place my hand against the side wall, then smell my palm. Mr. Ben's sweating, farting, belching sticks in the timber grain. Sure of it. I wonder if Ma Lexie will give me some paint if I ask nicely; a coat of paint will seal him in for good.

Empty bottles, old clothes, worn-down sandals. Why didn't he throw them away? What a pig. And the stink – I hold my hand to my face, breathe through my mouth. Has something died in here? Bet there's a dead mouse. A whole nest of dead mice. I check the hut's roof. Will it leak when it rains? Across the far end of the hut, there's a shelf with hooks screwed to the underside. I'll use them to hang up my clothes. I pick up a padlock from the floor, check which key will open it. I'll have no worries about my stuff going missing, about anyone poking around in my backpack.

I told Ma Lexie my documents were lost, but I still have them. Mother sewed them into the straps of my backpack. She made me sleep with my pack strapped with a belt to my arm, while she slept across the tent's entrance.

As soon as this place is clean, I'll unpack my winter clothes – could be too raggy to keep – my chess set, my comics. But still, I'm not sure the hut is a great idea. It's not just the smell I'm worried about. It's going to feel strange being on my own again, when the door's closed. There's no window. Should I tell Ma Lexie I don't want it? It reminds me too much of the tent.

In one way, I felt safe in the windowless tent. Anyone sneaking around the camp at night couldn't see me – see that I slept alone. But then, I couldn't see out. I spent hours wide awake – imagining people plotting on the other side of the tent's red fabric. I'd lie awake scared out of my head by each and every tiny noise. And that colour! Every morning, opening my eyes to a red world. Blue would have been better, the colour of the sky.

I back out of the hut, walk across to the edge of our flat roof. I grip the railing that runs the length of the knee-high parapet, and I gaze westward beyond the grey enclave, across the English border, to the distant mountains of Wales. I feel proud of myself for getting this far. My parents, wherever they are, would be especially proud of me today with my sudden promotion.

The birds will tell them. I wipe my eyes and glance back across my shoulder – no one's looking. My mother started all her tall tales the same way: "You know, Caleb, a sparrow came to my windowsill today, and she told me a strange tale…" A chiffchaff sometimes visited her windowsill, or a lark. As I grew older, I'd roll my eyes at her when she started like this. But I still liked to play along.

Mother had such plans for me, but I'm making my own future now – and it's nothing like her dream. She had our lives mapped out. Every night, along our journey through the Pyrenees, through France, we'd lie in the tent and she'd describe a new home, somewhere not too hot, not too dry. As if preparing me for disappointment, she'd whisper that our new home might be smaller than the one we left behind in Spain. First, she said, we would *introduce ourselves* at a reception centre – a doctor would check my health and give me the necessary inoculations. Better late than never, she said. I shouldn't complain if I felt sick for a few days because forced inoculation, she insisted, was the best indication that a country was worth reaching. In England, all children were inoculated at birth, with booster injections spread over time, a system that freed everyone from ever forming addictions – people were less violent, no compulsive gambling, no drug crime. Much safer.

"They don't need troublemakers, Caleb," she'd say. I tried to tell her that I wasn't a troublemaker, but she'd always shush me. When Mother disappeared, I had to make my own decisions.

I've been lucky, I reckon. Skylark found me on the road. She arrived pedalling a bicycle with a sidecar. She wore a leather jacket with a collar of long feathers – black feathers with shining glints of green. At that point, I'd joined a new group, and we were resting for a day. Skylark hung out with us all, let the children stroke her feathered collar.

I had a good feeling as soon as she told me her name. I could pass as her kid brother; she couldn't be much older than twenty. She was shocked I had no parent with me, said she'd take me under her wing. She laughed. It was a joke, she said – Skylark's wing. I impressed her with how I'd managed on my own for so long. When I explained I was heading with the others to a reception centre, she said *that* was the worst possible plan.

I have to admit, I didn't like the idea of those inoculations. Skylark told me: "I've never been inoculated. No way. You're as sick as a dog for weeks. It's best having the first injection at birth when the side-effects are negligible. And, you know, Caleb, you won't be the same afterwards." I remember she snapped her fingers twice in front of my face, and said, "You'll lose your spark."

Those reception centres, she told me, keep you for at least a year before handing you over to a work camp, and there were no schools on the camps as Mother thought. That came as a big surprise. Mother had it all wrong. Skylark said I'd be a slave for years in one of the many enclaves outside the big cities – doing filthy work on the fish farms and at the incinerators – and there's no guarantee of getting the right to stay.

Skylark offered to help me, but warned me not to tell the other people in my group, because she couldn't help everyone. She had space in her sidecar for just one, and she thought I had – what did she say? – *real grit*. She chose *me*. But the journey with Skylark was worse than I expected, and – if I'm telling the whole truth – once or twice I wondered if she'd tricked me. It was confusing; I thought Skylark wanted to rescue only me, but there were others, and we met up with them near the coast. She'd rescued all of them and I was the last to arrive. Once we'd crossed the Channel – the worst part, which I don't like to think about – everything happened so fast. Skylark dropped me off with Ma Lexie, and I haven't been hungry or cold since then.

I turn my back to the parapet railing and look over at the workshed. The kids aren't up yet. They'll be happy about my promotion, though I can't allow any slacking. I always tell them: the sooner they finish their work, the sooner they can play. But with Mr. Ben gone, they won't be afraid any more. Ma Lexie should find some older boys, like me, if she wants to make the business successful. Zach and Mikey are young for this work; they need too much help. And I know she never takes girls. Skylark told me so.

When Father finds me, or when I find him, he'll be impressed. I'm only twelve years old and I'm in charge.

I'm not sure how Father will track me down. Five weeks after he left, his messages stopped. Maybe he fell ill and he's in a hospital somewhere. At least we have a fail-safe. I'm sure he'll eventually return home, and I imagine the scene every night before I fall asleep. He'll open the tin – slotted into the stone wall surrounding the graveyard – and read Mother's message. I watched her write it: *We can't wait here any longer. If you've sent messages to us during the past twelve weeks, we haven't received them. We'll follow you to England – we'll be fine with Caleb's English. They won't turn us away if we accept indentured work. Then we'll find our compatriots in Manchester. We know you are safe. We feel it in our hearts.*

When I think of compatriots, I think of old people with white hair, sitting around with nothing to do. Drinking tea and complaining. I think I'm better off with Ma Lexie and the other kids. Ma Lexie says she's putting aside a little money each week for me, and when I'm fifteen she'll hand it over.

One day, definitely, I will find my family's compatriots. I'll have to tell them about Mother, about how tired she felt, and how she became confused and started sleepwalking. She disappeared one night. The people we were travelling with couldn't wait for her to return, but I refused to leave. I searched for days and days, looking in the hedgerows and ditches, but nothing. She didn't find her way back and, in the end, I had no choice. I sorted through her stuff and decided what to take with me. I traded her clothes. I unpicked the straps of her backpack, removed her documents and the last of our money. She told me at the start of our journey that money had only two uses until we reached Father – to buy food and to pay bribes. So, I took the money, a page from her passport, her sewing kit, and a photograph of my father, which would help me to trace him.

After three weeks without Mother, living and sleeping alone in my tent, I decided to join a small group of migrants who came through, heading north "towards kinder weather." Why fight the angry Gods, they said. My parents never talked about the Gods, but I didn't say so.

Skylark's eyes lit up when I said I used to help my mother with her sewing. She messed up my hair, laughed and said, "I've just the job for you."

I smile to myself because she was right; this job is perfect. It's hard work, but I don't miss school any more, only my friends. Yesterday, though, I nearly lost my nerve – pushing the needle through fur – it woke up memories, and the soles of my feet began to sweat.

I wash the keys and, in front of the two kids, I hang the keys around my neck. They grin, and Zach says, "I heard him leave last night! Gone for good?" Mikey offers a high-five, but I ignore him. "Hurry now. I'll bring breakfast. I want you both washed and dressed double quick."

As I slot the key into the stairwell door, I say to myself, the worst is over. Yesterday, I was one of the kids. Now, I'm Ma Lexie's right hand man. I pull open the door, lock it behind me and walk down the concrete steps.

There's another voice inside the flat besides Ma Lexie's. I

place my ear to the door. A man's voice. The same man as before?

When I first arrived at this housing block, hand-in-hand with Skylark – I stayed for three full weeks in Ma Lexie's kitchen. Never went out. Ma Lexie said I deserved a good rest, and I must eat three meals every day. She brought home a kitten for me to play with. And a man came to check my teeth. Another time, Ma Lexie came home with a woman – a nurse or a doctor – who told me to undress, down to my underpants. She checked me over and asked about the scar on my thigh. I told her it happened a long time ago, but I think she knew I was lying. I didn't want to talk about it.

Ma Lexie positioned my mattress in the kitchen so I couldn't see her bed from where I lay and gave me ear plugs so – as she said – she could have privacy. I knew what she meant because, on the road, I'd hear the night grunting and yelpy sounds from other tents. Those noises didn't bother me. But the ear plugs did – dirty with old ear wax. I used them all the same – scratched off the worst. After all, Skylark and Ma Lexie had saved me.

I knock and the boyfriend opens the door. He smiles and says, "Hello, mate. Long time no see."

Ma Lexie passes me the breakfast box and a flask. I try to look past her into the flat.

"Is the kitten here?" I ask. The boyfriend smirks, making me feel embarrassed. I'm the overseer and I shouldn't be asking about kittens. I say, standing to attention, "Thank you, Ma Lexie. I won't let you down. I'll do a better job than Mr. Ben."

The door closes and I hear the boyfriend laugh. I look down the stairs. I've never been in the stairwell alone. On Sundays, Mr. Ben took us down to the street, handed out pocket money and took us to a neighbouring block, to some relative of Ma Lexie's, an old man. He sold sweets and second-hand toys from the living room of his flat. One time, I persuaded Zach and Mikey to pool their money with mine, and we bought a pack of playing cards. It was worth it because the kids were getting so bored, and I was tired of inventing games. But they found it tough waiting an extra week for sweets.

I climb back up the stairs. One day, I'll have my own flat. I'll look out for my neighbours, make myself useful – and I'll win the janitor's job myself, like Ma Lexie. That's the easiest way I can see to get into business, because only a janitor can run a business on an enclave roof. All I'd have to do in return is brush and mop the stairwell, and wash down the solar arrays. I've already decided that I'll run a petting zoo on my rooftop or, even better, an aviary with cockatiels, budgies and lovebirds – a business I can run without any help. On the roofs surrounding Ma Lexie's, there's a laundry, a strawberry farm and my favourite – where Odette works – a garden with trellises, climbing flowers and bird baths. In fact, the bird baths are in my imagination, because I like to remind myself of the bird bath in the small garden at home. I haven't visited Odette's roof, but when Ma Lexie's in a good mood, I hope I'll persuade her to take me there. I guess she might be frightened because beyond the rooftop garden, on the next block, stand the *wretched beehives*, as she calls them.

Zach and Mikey watch me closely. The skin under Zach's right eye starts to twitch, and he lifts a finger to press down on his eye socket. He's worried, I guess, that I'll pick on him like Mr. Ben did. We sit outside the workshed on a raffia mat – a picnic, enclave style. I set out the flatbreads, the bruised apples, and I start pouring juice in our chipped beakers.

It's unfair to make the boys feel anxious, so I half-fill my beaker and fill each of theirs to the top.

"It's market day tomorrow, boys." They nod at me. "So we need to finish all the clothes on the table. Any problems – come to me. Let's not disappoint Ma Lexie. Hey?" They nod again. "Start on the easy jobs and make sure you finish them neatly. Push anything difficult to one side – I'll take a look at them this afternoon. I've a special order to finish this morning for Ma

Lexie. And don't forget to wash your hands after breakfast. Okay?"

"Mr. Ben is gone for good?" asks Mikey.

"Seems so. But we mustn't mess up. Or I'll be following Mr. Ben, and you two will be back on the street."

I take my drink and flatbread and pace the rooftop boundary. It's the only exercise I get. I lean over to check the street. Four floors below me, people are rushing to the shuttle station – off to Manchester, the city our enclave serves. I tried to tell Mother that I didn't want an office job. I wanted to be outdoors. After watching Ma Lexie, I've decided I want a life in business. I could be Ma Lexie's business partner. When she's old, I'll run the whole operation for her – choose the recycled textiles for our remake clothes, expand the team and build a fashion brand.

My plan is much better than Mother's. According to Mother, once we earned our right to stay, we'd take a flat in one of the enclaves, which are cheap because everything is subsidised for people who agree to live there. And then we'd find Father. When I turned eighteen, Mother said I could apply for an implant, cognitive chipping, and there'd be no looking back then. But how's that going to happen now, with two missing parents? I'll never gain approval for an implant – my family might be criminals, or politicos, for all that the authorities know.

Mother dreamed of a life one day in the city suburbs. She'd retire with Father and I'd support them. I'd be married in this dream, and my wife and I would be city workers. We'd all live together. But that was Mother's dream.

We work late every Friday, and today we're even later than normal. We've pressed all the finished clothes, folded them neatly into plastic containers, which are stacked ready for the market. Ma Lexie bangs on the steel door and I jump up to unlock it for her. She's carrying a deep bowl with our fish and rice supper.

This one day of the week, Ma Lexie sits at the worktable and eats with us. She serves. In silence – for we really are too tired to talk – we begin woofing down our meal. I glance around the table because, sitting quietly together like this, I imagine we look like a family.

Ma Lexie pushes away her empty dish. I stand up and start to clear the table, but she shouts, "Zach! You move the dishes. It's your job now."

I blurt out: "Let me do it one last time, Ma Lexie. Look how tired he is. He worked so hard today, believe me."

She stands up, folds her arms and glowers at the younger boy. "Do as I say, Zach." She leaves, and Zach takes our dishes to the rooftop sink to rinse them.

I collect my sleeping roll from the back of the workshed, push it under one arm and heave my backpack on my shoulder. Dragging a sweeping brush behind me, I tread past the solar arrays and approach the overseer's hut determined, even though I'm as tired as a dog, to sweep out the worst of Mr. Ben's junk. I'll push his junk into a pile, cover it with one of our tarps. Then I'll feel happy to move my stuff in tonight.

First, I dare myself to check the mattress. I stoop down, not too close, and breathe in. It's okay at the edge. I stretch across to the middle of the mattress. Still smells bad. I won't sleep on it tonight. I turn the mattress over so the other side will bake in the sun tomorrow. It might be okay by night-time.

As I straighten up, a plastic bottle clatters across the roof a metre behind me. Nice shot! I look across, wave to Odette and she waves back. She likes to send a message at this time of day. Almost a routine. I glanced across at her during the day as she served drinks to the garden's visitors. They pay a membership, and they expect good service. And there's such a long waiting list for membership that visits by each person can only add up to one hour a week. Odette keeps a record, and she's told me that everything in the garden has to be perfect every minute of the day – it's stressful.

I wish I could meet Odette face to face.

It isn't easy having a long-distance friend but we manage. We call across with one-word greetings. Mainly we throw messages in this short plastic bottle. We've put a stone inside; the extra weight helps. In fact, it took us a while to perfect our messaging method. Before we settled on this particular container and this size of stone, we lost a few messages when they fell short, ended up in the street. In those days, while we practised, we'd wait until the street was quiet before making an attempt. Anyway, Odette has the knack. Her throws are more accurate than mine. I like that about her.

I drag out Mr. Ben's chair, sit down facing Odette's roof and pop open the bottle's lid. I peer in – I'm being careful because last week I found a live beetle under her crumpled message. She won't catch me again. And I'm planning my revenge. I pull out the paper and flatten it against my thigh. Her written English isn't good: *Wats goin on your roof. I seen no fat man tday.* I reach over and grab a pen from the side pocket of my backpack. I correct her spelling when I reply: *What is going... I saw... today.* Then I write: *Mister Ben is history. He's gone for good. I am the new overseer.* She might not know the word overseer, so I add: *I'm the new Mister Ben. Going to market tomorrow with Ma Lexie.*

The label on the bottle – a smiling pickle – makes me laugh as I fasten the lid.

I take three strides backwards, imagine the flight path, run forward three steps and launch the bottle. Too far to the left, too high, it bounces on the parapet railing and drops onto the roof. Odette has her hands on her head. I hold out my hands. No sweat.

How old is Odette? I haven't ever asked, and she doesn't know my age either. Anyway, what does it matter? We don't have a street of friends to choose from. I haven't noticed anyone my age on any other neighbouring building. There's the old man who hangs out laundry, and the old woman who farms the strawberries. At a guess, I reckon Odette's older than me, maybe fourteen or even fifteen. When she finishes reading my note, she looks up and shouts, "Well. Done." She scribbles a note again and whirls around, readies herself and makes a short run up. She throws the bottle and I catch it. What a thrower!

The message reads: *Clever boy. Bring me a prez from the markit.* There's no space left for a reply, and I'm too tired to go hunting for another piece of paper. I wave, give the thumbs up and wave again.

Opening up my backpack, I dig out a roll of papers and add Odette's latest message to the top. It feels good to collect them together, as if I'm telling myself I can still make friends, given the chance. Flipping through them, I notice we never talk – I mean write – about the past. What's the point, and what can you write on the edge of some packaging material? If I had a whole sheet of paper I might tell her more. I'd like to tell her that my parents are educated – my father is an English teacher, and my mother a city clerk. In her spare time, she sewed costumes for the local amateur theatre group. My mother once complained that people assumed all the road walkers were poor, that we all left our homes because we had nothing to lose.

I sweep out the hut, throw my rucksack inside and fasten the padlock. My sleeping roll fits between the solar arrays – they'll offer a shield if the wind gets up during the night. Lying down, I feel peaceful for the first time today. The scar on my thigh starts to itch. I rub my finger along the lumpy line. It feels oddly soft.

After the first attack, Mother told me: "Those wicked people, they don't know anything about us. They attack the fear that lives deep inside, rotting them." In the middle of the night, they had rampaged through our camp, slitting open many of the tents. Mother and I woke when we heard screams, and we ran off. The young men and women in our group – those without children to defend – they ran at our attackers and fought in the mud. Afterwards, when we came out of hiding, we found that many of our companions were injured, and we did our best to help them.

The injuries were bad. Our camp cook was bleeding from a deep wound on his upper arm. Someone had stopped the blood flow with a belt fastened tight above the cut. But the wound needed stitching and we had no medic. At the start of the journey we had a midwife, but she left us for another group heading east.

My mother took control. She lit a fire and boiled water because, she said, everyone knows you have to boil water. She took out her sewing kit and, when the fire was hot, she held a needle in the hottest part of the flame. "The middle of the flame isn't the hottest," she told me. "If you put the needle there, it will come out covered in soot." I couldn't believe my eyes. She was totally focussed, so brave.

She said, "Find some spirits, Caleb. Vodka. Someone will have a bottle."

And that's when I started my first ever job – doctor's assistant. I watched her pour vodka over the wound, scissors and needle. She boiled the black thread. She examined the cook's torn flesh as I'd seen her in the past examining a ripped dress. She took her scissors and trimmed the ragged edges of his skin, saying, "Don't look away, Caleb. You should learn how to do this. Look here! I need a neat edge so I can close the wound properly."

Mother's sewing kit lies at the bottom of my backpack in a biscuit tin. A tin of chocolate fingers.

Mother became important in our group after that night. She began making rules. The young children had *not* to wander around barefoot when we camped. Otherwise, they had stupid accidents. When we made camp each night, she told everyone where to pile all our waste, so that sharp tins and bottles were out of harm's way.

The second attack came in daylight. We'd walked for days on quiet country roads surrounded by gentle rolling fields, which were muddied by early spring rainstorms. We could see for miles because the fields had no hedges. And we slept in small woods where we felt safer. We always cleared up after ourselves; we didn't want to annoy the farmers. But we couldn't avoid walking through one village and, looking back, we should have expected trouble. We rested in the village square while we took turns to fill our water bottles from a small fountain. No one shouted at us, but they all stared. Four men – looked like builders, muscular and tanned, one with paint splatters on his forearms – they stood close, legs wide apart, arms folded. Scowling.

We left as soon as we could. On the outskirts, a small van pulled up in front of us. Someone threw out a bin bag and sped off. My mother's friend poked the bag, looked inside and found a pile of stale bread and pastries, probably intended for a pigsty. But I thought it was kind, like someone cared. We shared them out.

A second parting gift came an hour later at a crossroads. A farm building hid our attackers from view. They came out holding knives. There were seven of them and I recognized the guy with paint splatters. House painter turned hard man. His arms weren't folded – he held an old shotgun, the barrel hinged open. Snapped it shut and shot above our heads. We scattered. I ran off the road, pulling Mother across the muddy field. They ran through us, pushed Mother to the ground. When they ran off, I saw my leg was bleeding.

I sometimes think that if I hadn't been injured, I'd still be with Mother. She couldn't handle it. She cleaned mud out of my wound and stitched it – twelve stitches in all – her hand trembling. She didn't *say* anything, but under the surface I think she freaked out. Me, being injured, losing blood. The skin didn't even need trimming, but the stitches were the worst ever. Other injured people needed help, but I saw she was struggling to keep a grip. We swapped jobs. I took the needle from her hand. *She* poured salty water on the wound – she'd learned that salty water worked better than vodka – and held the needle in the flame, while *I* stitched the wounds.

I made a bad job of the first one. Mother mumbled, as

though she really didn't care, that I'd trimmed too much skin away. We moved on to a man with a nasty slash across his back. He was hairy and the light was poor. I found it difficult to see exactly what I was doing as I pushed the needle through his skin, through his hair.

I couldn't help thinking of him yesterday when I stitched the fur collar – when I pushed my needle through the pelt.

A scream rips me from my sleep. I hear another scream. It's a cat fight. I open my eyes but I haven't escaped my dream. I followed muddy footprints on tarmac. And, in a ploughed field, I struggled to pin my tent across the furrows. Someone shouted, "Wolves."

It's true, we often heard animal cries at night. But I bet they weren't wolves.

I don't mind dreaming about the journey – I go there most nights – because now and then I see Mother as she used to be, before she became untidy and quiet. I roll onto my back, look up at the stars, and I hear her soft, clear voice from a time when everything was normal, when Father still lived with us: "Have you finished your homework, Caleb?" And then her voice is gone. I push myself up on one elbow, force my mind to clear.

I imagine the day to come – leaving the roof, walking through the enclave with Ma Lexie. I remember when I arrived here in darkness with Skylark – my surprise at seeing streets with no trees. It felt like a prison town without a perimeter wall. Blocks of flats, all the same size, separated by narrow streets and side alleys. Where I come from, every street was lined with trees, though many were dying back – bare branches poking out from the greenery, reaching for help.

Skylark led me up the stairs to Ma Lexie's flat and knocked. Ma Lexie let us in and, without being asked, Skylark filled the kitchen sink with hot water. She drew a curtain across the kitchen area, gave me a cloth and told me to strip off. "Time to clean up," she said. I must have stunk. I hadn't washed in hot water in weeks. I peeled off my sweater and two T-shirts, and Skylark – without coming around the curtain – handed me some clothes in a pile. I placed them on the floor away from the sink and smoothed my hand over the fresh clean cloth.

Above the sound of splashing water, I caught a few snatches of conversation – some talk about money, and I heard Skylark say, "... tall for his age." Ma Lexie asked, "Is he inoculated?" I didn't hear Skylark's reply, but Ma Lexie said, "Good. That's how I like them."

Before setting off to school, back home, I'd look down from our balcony, peer through the trees, to see if my friends were playing in the street. Often my friend Leo shouted from the street: "Come down, come down, Caleb. We need you." It felt good to hear that. But my parents didn't like me to play football before school. Instead, my father would test me on the vocabulary lists he gave me the night before.

Father walked me to school every day on his way to work. He would quiz me about my schoolwork because he wanted to get my brain started. He said I was too slow in the morning. I didn't like to tell him that I wasn't interested in many of my lessons. He wanted me to do well, but I knew I couldn't be like him. He once said, "You'll need to look after your mother and me one day. Our pensions will only cover the basics. It's your responsibility." I didn't understand him because I thought we were better off than most families. It was the first time he talked to me about money in a serious way. I wish I'd asked Mother on our long journey: were we poor? And, looking back, I think I was so used to walking with Father to school that it felt strange to find myself walking every morning, as a migrant, with Mother. I never got used to that.

I roll up my bedding, stand and stretch out my arms. If Ma Lexie sells my fur-collared shirt today... I'll be the apple of her eye. Maybe I was meant for this kind of life. Working with my hands, helping Ma Lexie in the market. I can't wait.

Suddenly, I jump out of my skin – a clattering. I swivel around and see a new message bottle by the hut's door. Why's Odette messaging so early? I pick up the bottle and look around, but I can't see her. I pull out an empty packet of marigold seeds, the sides are slit open, and inside there's a message: *In the markit, find me a small torch. Throw it to me tonite. Do not miss.*

Two

It's too damned quiet up there on the roof. Mr. Ben would be barging around by now, knocking stuff over, scraping back chairs. I look up at the ceiling. Come on, Caleb! Don't fall at the first hurdle, for God's sake. You need to prove yourself today.

I suppose he tossed and turned last night, over-excited about helping on the stall. But I shouldn't make excuses for him. He's got to pull his weight.

I hear the familiar creak-bang, creak-bang from across the street as Mr. Entwistle throws open his window shutters. I know it's nearly time for me to set off, because Mr. Entwistle is a man of routine. Same time each day, weekday or weekend – makes no difference to him. Naturally, I have my own routines, and I'm ready now, with the kids' breakfasts boxed up.

After living here for nigh on three years, I know the routines that punch through this building. On a weekday, I know it's time to haul my ass out of bed when my downstairs neighbour slams her front door shut. I know it's time for my second cup of tea when I hear the orange seller calling from the street. And I know I'm late taking the kids their breakfast when I hear my neighbour's chatterbox child on the stairwell, leaving for school with his quieter older sibling. I like to follow the young boy's fizzing monologue – picking up the odd word or two – as they leave the building and turn down the side alley.

The noisiest time on our street occurs shortly after nine every weekday – when the rubbish and recycling collectors lurch past with their bicycle trailers, and then empty the bins at the end of each block.

I don't let the boyfriend stay over on Friday night because of my early start. So Saturday morning is altogether quieter. I don't like it. Me, I need distractions – busy, busy, busy. No point dwelling on things, is there? Like how I miss my old life with Ruben, with our bigger flat, our parties. Like how my kid sister fucked up my chances, getting arrested for petty vandalism just before I was due for brain chipping. That's all it took for *me* to be judged an unsuitable candidate. Why would they enhance someone with suspect genes? The more I ranted my utter frustration the more my parents told me I was better off staying as I was, like them, fully organic.

Come *on*, Caleb. You'd better be up. Maybe he's creeping around trying not to wake the kids. I wouldn't be surprised. He's a considerate, sensitive boy. He's sunny too, which is surprising, even impressive. I pride myself that those three weeks he spent in my flat – eating well, playing with the kitten – helped him leave his past behind.

If I were more calculating – which I need to be, according to the family – I'd be more guarded. There's no doubt Caleb is a charmer, which can be a dangerous quality. It's easy for a charmer to morph into something darker, a trickster, a con-merchant. But the family can't understand; for me, the boy is simply nice to have around. He knows how to get on the right side of me. Acts more like an ally than... Well, he knows he's onto a good thing here.

He's probably up and ready, walking around barefoot, waiting for me.

I'll pay Skylark a bonus if Caleb comes good today. A

completion bonus; she deserves one not only for finding him, but for taking her time to persuade him. It's always better that way. They settle in quicker when they feel they've made their own decision. I hope Caleb follows Skylark's example, becomes someone I can trust, someone who's happy to work his way up.

When she delivered him, she gave me the backstory. She didn't overload me with detail; she knows I can't get involved with every kid. It's too draining. Apparently, Caleb set out with his mother, hoping to join his father who'd made the journey ahead of them. Same old, same old. Caleb told Skylark that his mother had sleepwalked, disappeared one night. He tried to find her, poor little sod. Skylark drifted around the small camp, spoke to others, tried to find out more about his mother, but no one knew much – Caleb had tagged along with them after his mother's disappearance. Skylark's best guess was that his mother suffered a breakdown, wandered off – died of exposure or something – or she was picked up, trafficked.

I haven't pried any further. He's the survivor type, and that's all that matters.

For once, I'll put my foot down with the family, tell them *I'll* make best use of Caleb. He'd be wasted in any other part of the business. In fact, I'll see Jaspar at the family premises later today and I'll bring up the subject. He makes all the big family decisions these days, so if I persuade *him* no one else will argue. The last thing I need is Jaspar nicking Caleb off me for heavier work. Caleb has more valuable skills. A case in point – that fur-collared shirt. Nice piece of work. But where did the idea come from?

I pick up the breakfast box for Zach and Mikey and head up the stairs. I unlock and push open the steel door. Soft morning light surges through the stairwell. It's quiet on the roof and the door to Caleb's hut is closed. Don't say he's still asleep. When I reach the workshed, I find him sat at the table, stitching. He looks up, flashes his smile and I melt. I leave the kids' breakfast on the shaded side of workshed.

"Look, Ma Lexie." He whispers, for the kids are still asleep.

"I'm covering these buttons with scraps of velvet."

"Leave that. Let's go. We'll get our breakfast in the market." He leaps to his feet. We each take two containers of pressed garments down to the street. I send Caleb back upstairs to fetch coat hangers and finally the tall hand-trolley. He runs up, two steps at a time, which makes me smile. Without being instructed, he stacks the containers on the trolley and grabs the handles. "What's the plan, Ma Lexie?"

"Follow me." I set out towards the market square.

The shutters are pushed back on my sister-in-law's ground-floor flat and I holler, as I always do, through the open window, "Amber!" After a few moments, she appears in the alley.

"Can't stop, Amber, I need extra time for setting up today." I point behind me with my thumb. "Meet my new overseer."

"Got a name?" asks Amber.

"Caleb, madam."

"Well, Caleb, you work hard for Ma Lexie today, and I'll invite you for tea and cake on your way home."

He looks at me, and then back at Amber, "I always work hard."

"It's true," I say. "And Caleb's pretty nifty with a needle and thread."

Amber frowns at me, and I know that look. She steps forward to hug me and murmurs, "Come on, Lexie. Let's avoid a re-run, shall we?" She pulls back and adds, "Come out tonight. Listen to the buskers, join the street dancing, hey?"

"No way. Not on a Saturday. I'll be wiped out." She doesn't press me. "Maybe tomorrow," I say. "I won't be so tired after the Sunday market."

We press on, and Caleb calls from behind. "Is she serious, Ma Lexie? About tea?"

"*She* is Miss Amber to you. Show some respect to my late-husband's sister."

"Husband? Late husband?"

I don't answer. For now, I must maintain the distance. As

the family keeps harking on: business is business.

Drives me crazy how they all watch me. Amber, no doubt, keeps them all informed, though she's kind enough. She knows the sacrifices I made when I married Ruben, that is, when I married *the family*. Even when my Ruben passed away, I didn't contact my parents. Why humiliate myself? They thought I'd married down, seriously down.

Since I was widowed, I admit that Ruben's family has been good to me – setting me up with the flat, the janitor's job and the remake business. It's small fry to them. I'm definitely grateful; it's not as though Ruben and I had any children. But the way they check on me… It's annoying, belittling. And I've no fucking delusions. If I ever re-married they'd take a different attitude. Kick me out of the flat most likely. So it's best to toe the line. And fair's fair – they don't mind the occasional boyfriend passing through.

"Ma Lexie? Who builds our stall? Did Mr. Ben set things up for you? Do I need to do that now? Is there a clothes –?"

"Too many questions."

The end of our street opens out into the market square with its food stalls, regimented into rows but precariously constructed – old doors and warped planks balanced on crates and blocks. The stall owners are piling up their produce, stringing up multi-coloured tarps to offer shade. I wave to the woman who sells fennel – another family widow. I love this time when the market belongs to the stall holders. No shoppers as yet, just the scrawny hangers-on who descend on the food stalls – youngsters mainly, trying to make themselves useful by tautening the canopies, hauling boxes of fruit and vegetables. All unpaid, working for tips. Entrepreneurs in the making, I reckon.

Today, though, I'm on edge. I'm going to put temptation in Caleb's path. Because I need to test his loyalty before I pull him closer. I need to know if he's playing me, if he's all empty charm. I walk faster, stretching the distance between me and the boy; he'll see that I trust him, and he'll taste a bit of freedom. I skirt around the food market and stop by the snack stall at the corner of Clothing Street. It's pushed tight against the end wall of a housing block. I daren't look around in case Caleb isn't there.

He appears beside me. Good, he wasn't tempted to run away. Maybe it didn't even occur to him. Gingerly, he tilts the trolley upright, with one arm stretched across the top container, stopping it from tipping forward. He looks up to me, expectant.

"Egg wrap?" I ask.

He nods. "With sauce," he says. "Please."

"Make that two egg wraps with the extras, and one with sauce," I say to the girl. She splashes oil in the wok, adds onions and herbs from two piles on the counter, cracks two eggs into the mix, whisks, adds spice. "And chilli," I tell her. She takes two thin pittas, spreads one with sauce and splits the egg filling between them.

We stand together eating our breakfast. My shoulders relax. As I look across the market square, I imagine a more traditional scene, with the addition of a church at the far end, and a fountain, and a statue of... anyone, for Christ's sake. Anything to relieve the back-to-basics look of the enclave. I mean, I know it's a cheap way to live, but does it have to look so bland? The enclave has its graffiti artists who've sprayed the end walls of the housing blocks, but it's all too loud for me. A single tall spire would make all the difference.

In Manchester, if I stayed after work for an hour or two, I'd say to a friend, 'Meet you by the Pankhurst statue'. I haven't visited the city since I married my Ruben. I gave up the job, and my free travel pass was revoked automatically. I've never missed the commute, the crammed carriages. And I haven't missed the job. Just another invisible organic working for the bright sparks, the clever bastards. Mind you, having worked with them, seen them up close, I don't envy them, not really. For all their brains – it's not even their *own* brains, it's brain chips making them supercharged – they're no better than skivvies themselves. Talk about a treadmill. They don't see it though, do they? Mind you, I wouldn't mind one of their fancy houses in the suburbs –

"Ma Lexie, do I still get pocket money? Or do I get a proper wage now?" He wipes his mouth with the back of his wrist, having finished his wrap already. I've no appetite; I hand him mine, half-finished. He takes it and starts chomping.

I laugh at him. "A wage? What are you worth, Caleb? More than Mr. Ben? Anyway, what do you need money for? I'm feeding you, aren't I? You've got a place to live."

"I think an overseer should get a wage. Not pocket money for sweets."

I laugh again. The cheek of him. Is he judging how far he can push? "You've a short memory. Hmm? Remember when you arrived here? Caked in dirt. Thin as a rake."

"That was then, Ma Lexie. I want to work hard for you, like your sis – like Miss Amber said. And I've plenty more ideas for the workshop, for new remakes."

"There's more to being an overseer than you realise. Mr. Ben made an early start on market days. He collected the boards and trestles from the family premises and set up the stall. I've had to pay one of the family's freelancers to do the job today. That's profit down the drain. You see? So don't talk to me about wages. You haven't proved yourself beyond a bit of handiwork. Be thankful for your breakfast treat."

The first of the shoppers are trickling in from the surrounding enclave when Skylark arrives at our pitch. I've finished setting out the garments on the table top, and Caleb, with his back to the street, is hanging the most expensive items on the clothes rail.

"What the hell is *that*?" asks Skylark, pointing at the fur-collared shirt.

Caleb spins around. "Skylark!"

"Come here, kid! I've missed your ugly mug."

They're in a bear hug as she says, "What are you doing out here? Got yourself promoted?"

He pulls away. "I'm Ma Lexie's right hand man."

She grabs him for another hug. "No, you idiot," she says. "I'm the right-hand man. Anyway, let's look at you." She steps back, looks him up and down. "Not as skinny." She leans in and inhales. "Smell a bit sweeter, too." She puts her arm around him, and it warms my heart to see Caleb so happy.

Skylark twists around and says, "Ma Lexie, I went to the premises yesterday. Your Mr. Ben's working on the separation line already." She snort-laughs. "I have to say, he didn't look happy. I couldn't resist – wandered over, all casual, asked him to pick out something nice for me, a fetching frock for a big night out. Told me to fuck off. Still has a way with words."

I turn to Caleb. "Don't just stand around. Tidy up the rails and fasten up all the shirts. They'll blow off the hangers if there's a gust of wind." Taking Skylark by the elbow, I guide her out of the stall, out of earshot. "How was the trip? Anything for me?"

"Sorry, nothing. Pretty tight family groups. A handful of singletons but they were all sick. Anyway, I thought you had enough with three boys."

"We'll see. I might need another, none younger than Caleb though. The young ones need too much organising. Listen, are you busy for the next hour?" Skylark shakes her head. "Take Caleb. Show him around – I'm cutting him some slack – and buy him a toy or a game. I don't know what kids want, and I can't leave the stall."

She gives me that *look*, the same as Amber's. She says, "There's no point spoiling him, getting too close. If Jaspar takes him off your hands like last time, you'll be crying in your soup."

I call Caleb over. Tell him to take a walk with Skylark. He hesitates, looks back and forth between me and Skylark, as if he's suspicious. I explain that I need the stall to myself for half an hour, that a business associate is calling by. I give him a handful of small notes, way more than the usual pocket money, and I watch him swagger away by Skylark's side. I wonder if Skylark has guessed I'm testing the boy. I want to know what he'll do –

money in his pocket, out in the market for the first time, his first real chance to make a run for it. After seeing him with Skylark, so relaxed, I reckon there's nothing further from his mind.

I hate it when people maul the goods. I can tell they won't buy anything. Take this young woman. Neat as neat can be, shy looking, but a sweet face. Somehow she manages to look down her nose at everything on display. And the lad who's with her, he's trying to cheer her up by injecting a little enthusiasm. Some folk are born miserable. She holds the cuff of the fur-collared shirt – hanging in pride of place – and she actually cringes. Her shoulders twitch.

God help us! No imagination, no sense of daring-do. What's the matter with people these days? It's all these damned inoculations – no one has any addictions, but these kids growing up now, they're all so damned... boring. With our remakes, well, I can read the confusion in people's faces. They don't know what they want until someone *like me* puts it under their goddamn nose.

The lad is still encouraging her to try something on. She picks up a cap made of army camouflage material with a fluorescent lemon peak – multi-coloured metallic beads sewn to the underside. Another of Caleb's ideas. He delegated the beading work to the kids.

She just stares at the cap. The lad takes it from her hand and puts it on her head. And she stands in front of my mirror, looking at herself, blank-faced. The cap suits her. The lad steps between her and the mirror, bends his knees. He pushes her hair behind her ears and pulls the peak down a tad and pushes it slightly sideways, as though the cap's accidentally off-centre rather than deliberately, cheekily cockeyed. He lifts her chin. It looks good on her. I'll offer a decent discount for the first sale of the day. But as I step closer, the girl casts the cap aside and they move on. Casts it aside! That's bespoke, lady. It's not jumble.

35

Speaking of which, I cast a glance farther along Clothing Street. On the opposite side, the second-hand clothes stall is as busy as ever. The clothes are thrown in heaps. But their profits per sale will be tiny compared to mine. I'm not interested in volume trade. I always told my Ruben, the family should develop more spin-offs from the recycling business. What's it called...? An add-on... No, *added value*. But Ruben didn't really listen. Not the listening type, was he? A real hard worker but, it has to be said, he liked a straightforward job.

God, I miss him though. If he could see me now with my own stall and all these remake fashions, he'd be proud. Ruben's mind fixated on one thing: the weight of recyclables – textiles, metals, glass, plastics, compost. I don't know why he worried. He told me himself that the weigh station staff were paid off. Boosted our weights by twenty per cent.

My Ruben saw himself as the family strong man – keeping rival clans off our street. He made his patrols after dark, checking every recycling bin from one end of our street, right across the market square, to the far end of the enclave. He said he needed eyes in the back of his head to stop other street clans pinching our stuff. He knew every bin on our patch, had them all marked, and checked none had been taken in the night. I imagine he was totally pumped up catching them red-handed – I've pictured him so many times. I see him, ploughing into them with his baseball bat.

Knifed through the heart for half a bin of metals. My Ruben, bless him, took the small stuff too seriously.

Three sales so far. I can't see far along the street; it's thronging. Where the hell are Skylark and Caleb? It's well over an hour since they left. I realise I'm nibbling at my lower lip.

Why do I do this – set people up to fail? People I actually do care about. Jesus, like that time as a teenager. I didn't remind anyone my birthday was coming up. My sixteenth. *Of course*, no one remembered. They were busy, working all hours. My parents felt terrible when they eventually noticed the date. Whereas, for me, I honestly don't know what felt shittiest – everyone forgetting my birthday, or seeing everyone's squirming guilt.

I like Caleb. That should be enough. He's well-adjusted and smart, strikes a positive attitude. There's no need to test him like this.

I'll tell the family through Jaspar, in case anyone's in any doubt, that I don't want to remarry. They'll appreciate that, a sign of respect for Ruben's memory. But I want a child – someone I can look after for a few years, who'll look after me in my old age. In fact, I could simply *do it*: move Caleb into my flat. I could build a platform above the living space for a mattress. I can't have him sleeping in the kitchen. The family will see how happy I am, and Jaspar might be prompted to give me a bigger flat. Or he could encourage the tenant next door to move on, and then knock through. That would be grand. Jaspar could make that happen.

Anyway, the family will realise soon enough that something's afoot. Mr. Ben being demoted, Caleb coming to the market. Amber's bound to mention Caleb at the Sunday gathering. Yes, I'll tell Jaspar today that I want to keep Caleb. I'll *tell* him. I won't ask.

I catch sight of Skylark edging, shoulder first, through the crowd. I take payment from a young man for a pair of shorts with bespoke trim on the side seams and pocket edges – a quick job, five minutes with the machine. I fold the shorts, tie them with a thin strip of cloth to make a handle. He doesn't seem too impressed, but it's all part of the service. As he leaves, Skylark darts between the stalls. She's on her own.

"I lost him. At the toy stall in the next street."

"How could you lose –?"

"He ducked down to look in a box of oddments. I don't know, maybe he crawled under the stall and ran from the back end. Couldn't see him, chased up and down, but –"

"He ran away?"

"He might be lost, or... How much money did you give him?"

"It's only enclave credits; he won't get far –"

Skylark lays her hand flat on top of her head. "But he seemed happy. Why run away?"

"Because no one knows who he is yet. It's his first day off the roof. In a month's time everyone will know he's with me."

"Let's not panic. If he's lost, he'll find his way back to the food market and –"

"Yes, he'll find his way from there."

"I'll keep searching, Ma Lexie. I'll go to the market square, and if he isn't there I'll check if he went home."

As Skylark turns, Caleb crashes into her. "Sorry, Ma Lexie. Sorry. I looked up and I panicked. I couldn't see Skylark." He looks up at her. "Where did you go?"

I lean over and pull him by his top around the table.

"Sorry, Ma Lexie," he whines.

I slap his face.

My mother slapped me often enough. It's not the end of the world. But Caleb's been sulking for the past half hour and won't look at me. I sent Skylark to fetch him some sweets, but he hasn't touched them. Pushed them in his pocket. I'm festering now with the worst doubts. Did he try to run away but chickened out? I don't know what to think. Did he take his chance and then realise he didn't have a plan? Will he spend the next months working out how to get away? I don't want to be suspicious; I want to believe he lost sight of Skylark and panicked, as he claimed.

We go on like this until late morning: there's me, acting as though nothing has happened, chatting with the customers, pretending Caleb isn't even there; and there's Caleb, standing at the back pretending he's invisible. One of my regulars turns up and we have a laugh. I want Caleb to see that people like me.

A guy I haven't seen before strides up to the stall, points and asks about the shirt. What kind of fur is it? I tell him it's mock. And he asks, mock-what? I make something up – mock arctic fox, I tell him. He says he's doing a music gig, and he'll take it; it's different. I tell Caleb to wrap it nicely. He's watched me wrapping other items, and I reckon he'll enjoy his first sale, if he can get over himself, stop his sulking. He hands over the wrapped shirt and smiles, just about. As the guy heads off, Caleb takes out his sweets and starts to suck on one.

By two o'clock the market is thinning, and I tell Caleb to start packing away. I tell him we've had a good day, thanks to his creative flair. He takes the compliment and once again tries to smile. It's more like a twitch. I wonder if his face is stinging.

I take a deep breath. "Caleb. Listen to me. I won't hit you again. I was worried and... you know, I don't want you to disappear like that. Gave me a fright." I add, "You're important to the business. So from now on, you'll have a wage instead of pocket money."

He nods his head.

I think we're over the worst.

I say, "We'll go home via the family premises. But first, go back to the fruit market and fetch three pomegranates – a treat for you boys. Go to the woman with the rose tattoo on her throat. Tell her Ma Lexie sent you. And while you're doing that, I'll finish the packing."

I watch him flip-flop down the street. I must be mad, testing him again. But I want him to make good his wrong.

We walk back along Clothing Street with the trolley. Instead of turning left towards our housing block, I turn right towards the family premises. At the far end of the street, the housing blocks give way to a shamble of workshops with perimeter walls, and storage lock-ups, mostly built from recycled plastic building blocks, with battered wooden or steel gates. No signage. Around here, enclave entrepreneurs like to keep a low profile. But the recycling business is different – public contracts and all that – and as we approach the compound walls, I point Caleb to the sign:

Materials Recycling Facility
Enclave W3
No Dumping

"You'll get to know this place, Caleb. It's the family HQ. We keep our bicycle trailers here for the bin collections along our street. And it's the sorting facility for recyclables from the entire enclave – we won the contract a few years back. The family's doing well." I place my hand on his shoulder. "Stick with me and you'll never be short of work."

I look up at the camera and the gates' unlocking mechanism clunks.

"What happens to the rubbish, the stuff you can't recycle?" Caleb asks. I smile. He seems to be perking up.

"We don't bring it here. It's biked out to the incinerators on the eastern edge of the enclave."

The yard is deserted at first sight. The bicycles and trailers are parked up against the perimeter wall. But then I notice there's a mechanic tinkering with one of the bikes. I avoid coming here during the week when it's chaotic. Fact is, if I'm being honest, I don't like seeing the kids who've worked for me – the ones Jaspar has purloined. Makes me feel bad they're doing such dirty work. Within months they're hardly recognisable. They change shape, with all the cycling and heavy lifting. At least if they're on the collection side, they're not sorting in the warehouse – too hot in the summer, too cold in the winter – and it's pure bedlam in there with the conveyors, rolling drums, air blowers, sorting screens. Last time I went in, I threw up.

"Caleb, I need to talk business with my brother-in-law. You run over to the warehouse, have a rummage in the textile bay." I point to the near-end of the warehouse. "There's a security guard. Say you're here with Lexie."

He looks up at me, quizzical. "Have a rummage?"

"It's part of your new job. Bag up the best and we'll take it home. Don't see why I should do it any longer. I couldn't ask Mr. Ben to do it; he had no idea. So… off you go."

"But how much –?"

"Whatever you can balance on the trolley."

I head off towards the office – a windowless steel shipping container. We keep a strongbox welded to the floor, and it's the safest place to leave my takings. I don't leave cash lying around at home. I've gleaned that my latest Romeo has a limited understanding of 'what's mine isn't yours'. He's had the nerve to drop hints about moving in with me. The next thing you know, he'll be saying, 'let's share and share alike'. I don't care that he's lazy, so long as it doesn't affect me. I'm nobody's meal ticket. My Ruben would climb out of the grave.

Jaspar steps out of the office, looks across at the warehouse as Caleb parks his trolley and disappears inside. "Who's the kid? I could do with an extra pair of 'ands on the sorting line. When's the 'andover?"

"He's too smart for this work, Jaspar. He's better staying with me. He's doing nice work, proper designer in the making."

"Fancy that," he says, all sarcastic. He smirks. "*This,*" – he waves towards the warehouse – "*This* is where the family makes its money. Where there's muck etcetera. Yer *operation,* if I may raise it to that lofty status –"

"Don't patronise me, Jaspar. If you need more hands, tell Skylark, and pay her a bonus if she delivers."

"Just sayin' – Keep yer 'air on."

"Well, I'm telling you, the boy's staying with me. I'm paying him a wage from today, so don't fucking mess with my plans."

He rolls his eyes. "Calm it, will yer? And this is strictly business, is it? I mean, if I took 'im off yer 'ands, would we 'ave them tears again?"

"That was two years ago. I was still in a bad way after Ruben. So, hands up, I over-reacted." I pass the takings to him.

He retreats into the office, and I call after him. "I admit, I like this boy, but it makes real business sense to keep him."

"I've told yer: Don't mix business and personal shit."

"It's all right for you, Jasp. Married with four lovely kids. My marrying days are over. Ruben was the only one for me." I hate to use Ruben like this. It's still difficult for his family, especially for Jaspar, losing his kid brother.

After Ruben's murder, the enclave police weren't too bothered about following up – regarded it as clan business – so we did our own investigating. Asked every resident what they'd thrown in the stolen metals' bin, and we made an inventory of everything the residents could remember. Jaspar's unloading team at the yard inspected every delivery of metals for weeks and weeks against that inventory. Four months on, we spotted a small wire sculpture of a dog that some old fella had made and discarded to the stolen bin. Jasper went to see him with what we'd found, and he confirmed it was the one he'd chucked away. According to the delivery records, the wire dog arrived at the recycling yard from the far side of the enclave, from a collection gang that had *previous form* for pilfering, according to Jaspar. By then, the police had long forgotten about my Ruben. They didn't make the connection when the retributions started. More than one tit for one tat. But that's how it goes.

Jaspar locks the strongbox, and continues his needling. "We don't want no embarrassment for the family. The kid's a migrant, could be anyone. Yer've no idea what he's gone through, what he might do. Might be a ticking time bomb for all we know. And I'll tell yer another thing for free." He steps towards me and grabs my arm tight, doesn't let go. "I don't like that fuckin' loser yer seein'. Don't look good." He juts out his chin as though spoiling for a punch. I come dangerously close to laughing at the jerk, even though he's hurting me. He lets go of my arm. God, it stings.

"I'm finishing with him, Jasp. I just got lonely…"

"Don't *you* finish with the loser. *I'll* put him straight. We don't want no shouting match for the neighbours to blab about. Do we?"

"And I can keep the boy?"

"Yeah. Keep the little bastard, if he's that special."

Caleb returns from the warehouse with two large bundles of clothing, one gathered up in a blanket, the other in a torn sheet. He balances them precariously on the trolley, and it's obvious I'll have to carry one of them. I wonder if his face will be bruised by morning.

"Why so much, Caleb? That's easily twice as much as we need for one week."

The bundles slip off.

"It's a new idea, Ma Lexie." He still sounds a bit downbeat, but at least he's talking.

"Please do share," and I'm surprised at the sarcasm in my voice. Jaspar brings out the worst in me. I add, trying to sound calm, "I'd like to know."

"I'm going to cut up eight or nine pairs of trousers to make one or two pairs of remake trousers."

"What?"

"They're worthless right now."

"Why nine pairs – surely two or three – swap the pockets, that sort of thing?"

"This is different. I'll cut them in curves and piece them together like a curvy-edged jigsaw."

"Too much stitching."

"It's all machine work. No hand-stitching."

"Make the fur-collared shirts first. After that, I'll give you one day to make a sample for me. *One day*, are you listening? Then I'll decide if we'll begin a new line." As an afterthought, for I can see his face is indeed still red from the slap, and his forehead is creased as though he has a headache, I say, "I'd like to start a new line of specials. I'll give you one day every week for developing new ideas. Agreed?" He nods and, at last, a smile, though he's still frowning. "We'll get the kids to make labels and stitch them on the outside of the clothes." I turn towards to the metal entrance gates, and so I don't see his reaction when I say, "We'll call it the Caleb fashion line."

He doesn't reply.

There's a ruckus outside – kids screaming, playing some stupid chasing game. I walk on ahead, back towards the centre of the enclave, but I twist around because I can't hear the trolley squeaking. He's standing there, just staring at the kids. They're chasing one another with sticks, there's a ball in there somewhere, and they're kicking up clouds of dust.

I call to him. "Come on. Remember? Cake?"

I'm too tired to walk to the shower block down our street. I close the kitchen shutters, strip off and fill the sink with warm water. Caleb's gone back to the roof with the food we picked up on the way home, and he also took the pomegranates. It occurred to me that I should take the keys away from him, but I'm pretty sure I can trust him. He seems keen about the remake trousers. And I don't want him to feel demoralised, which he would be if I took the keys. I have to assume, for the time being, that he told the truth about losing sight of Skylark. He panicked, that's all.

I'm free for the rest of the evening. I should be happy with the day – trade was good, and Jaspar agreed to let me hold onto Caleb. What's more, I have the beginnings of a real plan – a new line in remakes. I'll sketch some ideas for the label's design. Could be the start of a bigger business. In fact, I see no reason why I shouldn't expand, supply other enclaves. If the business does take off big time, I'll give up the janitor's job. It makes far more sense to rent a workshop near the family premises.

I take my washing cloth, an old thin hand-towel, and soak it in the warm soapy water. I wring it, but not too tight, shake it out and throw it across my back. A satisfying slapping sound bounces off the kitchen walls. Pulling the cloth back and forth, I start to feel cooler. Slowly, I wipe myself down. I stand still enjoying the goosebumps. Leaning over the sink, I rinse my face with fresh water from the tap, pull a strand of hair across my face and inhale. The bad-sweet smell of the recycling yard lingers. I put my head under the running tap.

I sit cross-legged on my bed. The bed sheet is scattered with dashed-off sketches for a "Caleb" logo. He'd like this one. I pick up the outline of a leaping cat.

At Amber's place this afternoon, he instantly recognised her marmalade cat when it jumped in through the window from the street. There's no mistaking its markings – a white front leg and white chest. Caleb pointed, dumb, his mouth full of cake. I explained, "Yes, I borrowed the cat while you settled in. But she lives here."

I couldn't believe it. His eyes filled with tears. Acted like a baby. He slid down on to the floor and played with the cat for the rest of our stay. I felt embarrassed by him, so I deflected Amber before she passed comment. I could see the start of a sneer. I leaned towards her, told her my boyfriend was getting his marching orders, that Jaspar insisted on 'handling the situation'.

She said, "That's probably wise."

Caleb wasn't paying us any attention. Amber shifted closer and told me she'd never liked the boyfriend, thought he was annoyingly flippant, as though he didn't need to earn a living like everyone else. Got up her fucking nose, she said, the way he took advantage of my good nature. "You've got to stop this – always seeing the best in people."

I said, "Well, I didn't make a mistake with your brother Ruben, did I?" Which she could have taken as a compliment if she cared to. I was past caring. I mean she'd never piped up about lover boy before now.

No point getting het up. I know I've had my best years.

I never felt too tired to go out dancing with Ruben. I feel his hand on my waist and glimpse the roll of his hips. He was some dancer!

In reality, I had no great qualms walking away from my own family, though I never thought I'd end up here. Like this. If we'd had children, I might have patched things up with my own parents. I suppose it's possible they're looking, even now, to end the rift. People can't stay angry for ever.

Unless they don't even think of me. I draw an outline of a cat with a bird in its mouth. I might be dead to them already.

Three

As Zach spreads out the raffia mat, Mikey fires questions at me about my first day off the roof. He wants to know how far it is to the market, if Ma Lexie let me serve on the stall. And he pesters me to ask Ma Lexie if he and Zach can go next time. As I answer one question, he's interrupting with the next. I hold my hands up to say, 'Enough'.

Zach chips in with a single question: did I see any stalls selling figs? I'm not surprised by his question. He told me one time that his family had fig trees, but when I asked how many, he didn't know. It's possible his family owned an entire fig farm. *Or,* just as likely, Mikey remembered a small garden at his family home – two or three fig trees planted for shade as well as fruit. I felt sad that he remembered so little. I explain to Zach, that I didn't have time to look around the fruit stalls, but there must be figs somewhere, and I'll try to buy some at tomorrow's market if Ma Lexie lets me.

He says, "I like figs more than sweets."

We sit ourselves down, picnic-style again, and I hand out the spicy egg wraps. It was my idea to buy the street food on our way home. I told Ma Lexie, "You must be too tired to cook. You've had a busy day." In fact, I couldn't care less about Ma Lexie being tired. I was worried about Zach and Mikey who would be starving hungry. During the weekend markets, they go without food at midday – there's no one around to feed them. So, buying street food was simply the quickest way to get the kids fed.

I put on a brave face – same as I did at Jaspar's recycling yard – because I can't admit to the kids that I've been in trouble with Ma Lexie. I pretend everything's okay by telling them about the amazing sight at the far end of Clothing Street. I saw it when I walked through the market with Skylark: a massive pink sheet was strung up between two buildings on opposite sides of the street. It blew around in the breeze high above the stalls, like a giant advertisement saying: *Welcome to Clothing Street.* I explain to Zach and Mikey that most of the stalls sold second-hand clothes, piled high, but Ma Lexie's stall looked special. "We should feel proud of that," I say, making a real effort to sound happy. My fur-collared shirt, I tell them, sold to a musician for a sky-high price and he didn't even barter.

And I give them the gossip, that Ma Lexie was married one time, that she's widowed now.

I describe Miss Amber's flat and the cat with the incredible coat of fur – orange with one patch of white on its front leg. I told them I'd seen the cat before, when it was smaller, when I first arrived at Ma Lexie's flat. I tell them that I'm sure the cat remembered me because she curled up in my lap like we were old friends. But I don't tell Zach and Mikey about Miss Amber's cake because I don't want them to feel jealous.

And I don't tell them that Ma Lexie hit me.

I've never been hit across the face before. My parents never ever smacked me. The inside of my mouth still stings, but at least I can't taste blood any longer. After the slap, Ma Lexie joked around with her customers as though nothing had happened, and Skylark gave me toffees. Did Skylark really think that toffees would make everything all right? I thought I'd be sick if I tasted anything sweet, but in the end, my mouth was hurting so much I tried one, and it did ease the pain a little. Then, out of nowhere,

Ma Lexie said she wouldn't hit me again. I wanted to tell her that no one in my family ever hit another person, that she was bad.

Instead, I clamped my mouth shut, and I imagined a blade in my hand. I saw myself lunging at her. And I know I'll be ready, if only with my fist, if she ever does that again, in front of people, in front of Skylark.

I expected a telling-off after I gave Skylark the slip, but Ma Lexie should have believed my story. So I learned an important lesson today. It took me a while to work it out. My head was ringing. While I stood at the back of the stall, I decided Ma Lexie didn't trust me – even though I'd worked hard and tried to be jolly all the time. I never once blamed her for any of my problems. I decided, standing there listening to her laughing and joking with her scummy customers, that Ma Lexie might be just another chapter in my story of hard luck.

When I saw the cat at Miss Amber's, I lost it, as though I couldn't hold back all the sadness. I had to dive off my chair to hide my tears. What with Ma Lexie hitting me, and with the warning from the guard at Jaspar's warehouse. The guard said, "Don't get too cosy with that boss of yours. The last one she took a shine to was *confiscated* by Jaspar. Ended up 'ere on the sorting lines. But the kid got right up Jaspar's nose. Shipped 'im out."

I don't know why, but I said to the security guard, "Thanks for telling me." And he replied, "No skin off my nose."

As usual when we sit on our mat, I make sure I'm facing Odette's roof. I like to watch her move in and out of the garden as she takes drinks to the visitors. When she isn't busy, she stands quietly, all watchful, and I'm sure she chooses a place to stand where she can look across to my roof. One of the things I really like about her, at least from a distance, is that she always looks so clean. Her dark hair is neat, scraped back in a ponytail.

I stand up. "Save the pomegranates for later, boys, or you'll be hungry again before bedtime."

Mikey clears away the food wrappers, and Zach rolls up the

mat while I walk across to the edge of the roof and wave to Odette. She doesn't move. I guess she's being careful, in case her boss or the visitors are watching her. So I head off to the workshed to sort through the recycled clothing I brought home from the warehouse. While I'd rummaged in the textile bay, I'd picked out two warm tops for myself and buried them deep in the bundles. I've learned to plan ahead like this. The days will be getting shorter soon, and with these warm clothes I won't wake up in the night, freezing cold.

I carry the tops back to my hut and hang them from the hooks under the shelf. I like the look of them. It's good to have something new.

I take off my T-shirt and wash at the sink. It's odd; it's a relief to be back on the roof where I can reach up and almost touch the big blue sky. Down on the street – this came as a surprise – I felt the buildings were leaning in, that they could easily topple over and bury me.

As I turn away from the sink, I see Odette, waving – not in a 'nice to see you' way, but in a way that says 'hurry up, I need you'. I cock my head. What's the big panic? She pretends she's throwing a bottle and waves towards herself.

She wants the torch, but why the drama? I should tell her about the trouble her stupid errand dropped me in.

Skylark took me to the toy stall, and on the way I saw a pile of gadgets, mostly junk, and I spotted a solar torch. I should have told Skylark I wanted to buy it, but something told me to keep quiet. I mean, why did I want a torch? If she'd asked me, I didn't have an answer for her. Because, here on the roof, there's light from the street lamps. And I couldn't say I wanted the torch for Odette – Skylark would have too many questions about that!

When we reached the toy stall, I waited until Skylark looked away, and I ducked down, retraced our route, bought the torch and ran back. I'd been gone for a couple of minutes, that's all, but

Skylark had disappeared. I raced around the stall, looked down an alley that led away from the market, hoping to catch sight of her. The alley stretched away into the distance. I don't know why I did it, but I took a few steps, and then I ran as though the alley was sucking me along.

I just wanted to run, maybe to find the end – where the enclave meets the countryside. It felt good – to be on my own, and running. I reckon I'd run half the length of the alley when I came to my senses and ran all the way back, straight to Ma Lexie's stall.

I wrap the torch in a cloth, push it into a wide-necked container and add more padding for a snug fit. On a scrap of paper, I write, *What's the panic?* The container is heavier than the usual bottle. Odette's waving, encouraging me to throw. I hold it up and gesture that it's heavy. She puts her hand to her forehead; she thinks I'll fail. I practise a longer run-up, and feeling confident, I run – counting the steps – and launch the container, higher than usual.

She reaches and with her fingertips she manages to break the container's fall. She rushes off, out of sight, and I'm left wondering what she's up to. I sit and watch.

The sun is low, and I'm ready to flop out. I can hear Zach and Mikey playing at the far end of the roof. I'm relieved they haven't pestered me to join in. I'm suddenly reminded of the older boys and girls playing outside the family premises this afternoon. As soon as I heard them screaming for the ball, memories washed over me. For a couple of seconds, I was standing in my street back home, on the sidelines watching my friends running around. It was a long time since I'd seen a sweaty, shoulder-barging, shirt-grabbing ball-game of any kind. But it hit me that this enclave game had a nasty edge to it. Each kid had a stick like a stripped branch, and it seemed – but it was difficult to believe – that they were using them to hit *one another* rather than

51

the ball. I'd never seen anything like these sticks – hand-painted as if in team colours, either pale blue or yellow, with coloured stripes around the shafts.

Still no sign of Odette. I may have missed her; there's only the street light now. I thought she'd send me a message, thank me for the torch. She hasn't even asked how much I paid for it. Unless she thinks I stole it. I guess she wants a torch for when the days become shorter. Maybe she wants a better light for reading. Or she's afraid of the dark, and when autumn comes – when it's too cold to sleep under the stars – she plans to fall asleep in her hut under torchlight. I can't blame her; since I crossed the Channel to England, everyone sea sick, in total darkness –

The steel door creaks open on her roof, and I see the silhouette of Odette's boss, a stooped woman who always dresses in black. I think she's carrying a plate of food. She disappears into the garden. I guess she'll leave Odette's meal near her hut.

After a couple of minutes, she hasn't reappeared. They must be chatting. Thinking about it, Odette has never said anything about her boss in her messages, nothing good, nothing bad. I suppose that means her boss is okay.

I decide to crash out, accepting that Odette will chat away the entire evening without messaging me. As I turn away, I catch, in the corner of my eye, a darting movement on her roof. I look across. She darts again, stops suddenly and runs in my direction. She throws a bottle and it flies way over my head, landing on the far side of the roof. Ha, she's overdone that! I chase across and find the bottle perched over the roof drain. I use two hands to lift it, carefully – I don't want to nudge it down the drain. I'm still feeling pleased with myself as I open the bottle and read the message: *I am leeving NOW. Going to the hills. Come with me. Only 1 chance.*

I'm staring, my chin pulled in, reading and re-reading these four strange sentences.

Going to the hills?

I see myself sprinting down the alley this afternoon. It felt good.

Only one chance?

I probe the inside of my cheek with my tongue. It still hurts. Ma Lexie hit me hard. And I know she'll do it again.

All's quiet in the workshed. I glance across. I can't help Zach and Mikey. I mean, I just *can't*.

And *if* I'm going to run away, I know what to take.

Odette approaches the rail, and I walk forward so we face one another. She raises her hand and spreads her fingers wide. I think she's *signalling*... five minutes.

I return the signal and feel every hair stand on end. I imagine meeting her in the street. I'll see her smile, close up.

There's a sudden buzzing in my ears and it's deafening. I swallow hard. My legs are heavy, as if my feet are caked in mud. I walk slowly towards my hut even though I haven't made up my mind; I can decide while I'm packing.

It's a lesson I learned on the road. When there's an emergency, the ones who survive best are the ones who think and act immediately, who don't wait to see what other people do. I'm tipping everything out of my backpack as I focus my thoughts on winter weather, cold nights, wet feet. Before I start to repack it, I change my shorts for trousers, flip-flops for socks and shoes. Into the backpack, I place the two warm tops – Odette might need one – Mother's sewing kit, a spare pair of shoes. I step outside, go around the back of the hut and pull out, as quietly as I can, a scuffed green tarp, and I fold it. I place it inside the backpack as an extra waterproof layer – an old habit – to protect my clothes. I add my hat even though it's smelly, all my socks and a couple more T-shirts. Almost done. I have one thin plastic cape, which I fold and push into a side pocket. I've no food, only a pack of toffees. But I have money in the straps of my pack, and I pray that Odette is better prepared.

I sit and hug my pack. My eyes are closed.

I find myself on my feet, my pack over my shoulder, and I'm stepping out of the hut. I shut the hut door so it doesn't creak or bang shut during the night. There's an empty bottle by the parapet wall. I take it over to the sink and fill it with water, push it in a side pocket.

My ears are still ringing. Five minutes must be up by now, but I can't see Odette. I haven't heard her opening the steel door. Maybe she can see me – our roof is more open than theirs. I remove my shoes and tiptoe across to the workshed. There's no sound coming from the kids, and when I look in, I see their body shapes under their blankets.

The question is, can I unlock the steel door and open it without alerting Ma Lexie? The sound of women laughing and shouting reaches me from somewhere in the neighbourhood. I wait, rest my head against the warm steel. When the women reach our building, still shouting, I turn the key and ease the door open. I'm standing in the stairwell. It's open at ground level to the street – there's no entrance door on any of the enclave housing blocks – which means there's nothing but fresh air between me and the street. The women's laughter echoes up the stairwell and slowly fades. If Ma Lexie has heard a suspicious noise, she'll be listening carefully. So I don't lock the door behind me. Quickly, gripping my shoes, I pass Ma Lexie's flat. Down, down, and one flight from the entrance, I stop, push my feet back into my shoes and wait.

I could turn around even now.

If Odette isn't waiting for me, I'll go back. The door to the roof is still unlocked. Ma Lexie wouldn't hear anything.

From the street, I hear "Caleb!" I can't see her, but I rush down the final steps. She appears at the entrance, a face of stone, and with a head jerk, tells me to follow. Not as prim-looking close up. Her ponytail is skew-whiff and strands of oily hair have come loose.

Four or five paces behind her, I'm panicking – we look all wrong. Me with my backpack, wearing trousers and shoes on a hot night, and Odette with a small but bulging bag with a long strap digging into her shoulder. She's wearing a dress and flip-flops, not exactly escape gear. I've got a bad feeling.

There's an alley up ahead leading off the street. I rush forward, grab Odette's arm and pull her into the alley, saying, "I'm known down that street – Ma Lexie's sister lives there."

"Okay, okay," she snaps. "But we must go in that direction soon." She looks at me. "You're younger than I thought."

"So where…?"

"Head south, find the canal path, head to Wales. You're my half-brother – got it?"

I'm relieved. She has a plan, and a story. "Got any food?"

"Some. Enough."

There's a lump deep in my chest. "Let's run."

"No! Look normal."

"What do we say if –?"

"No one's going to stop us. It's Saturday night. The police stay close to the market square."

"How did you get away? I didn't see your boss."

But she ignores me. "Walk slowly – like we're tired, near the end of a long walk." After a few seconds, "Thanks for the torch."

"How far is Wales? Where –?"

"Not sure. We'll walk at night, sleep during the day."

"But what happens in Wales? I mean, is it any better than here?"

She ignores me again. "Let's go another two blocks down the alley then turn south."

"But, how do you know where the canal is?"

She keeps her head down as she says, "People come to the garden. They chat. One old man worked on the canals, talks about the old days. I know if we walk south we will find a canal."

"We won't miss it?"

"Impossible. There are two canals that meet and the enclave sits in a 'V' between them. See? It's simple, we keep walking south, across two or three fields."

Two or three fields doesn't sound too bad. And now I click – it's totally sensible to leave in the summer, in dry weather. We've had no rain for over three weeks. It's a clear night, too, so we'll follow the stars like Mother and I did. Odette turns off the alley. The enclave is built on a grid and this street will take us well away from the market square.

We've been walking for at least twenty minutes. We've passed a few people but no one has paid us any attention. I'm beginning to think this is easy when three men exit a building about fifty paces ahead of us, and even at that distance I see their swagger. So does Odette. She takes my elbow, pushes me through the entrance to a block of flats and marches me up the first flight of stairs. She whispers, "Wait." She's still gripping my elbow, as though I might run off, but when the men have walked by, she releases me and we set off again.

She stops when we reach the last housing block. Before us lies a mess of workshops and shacks, with no street lights.

"Watch for dogs," I say. "Pick up a stick if you see one."

Dropping her bag to the ground, she pulls out a dark sweater, full of holes, and pulls it over her head. She pulls on baggy black trousers, swaps her flip-flops for shoes and tucks her dress inside the trousers.

While she's doing this, I'm losing my nerve. I'm confused. Why did she ask me to come with her? Am I being stupid? She's not my friend, not really – not like a friend back home. Also, she's older than I thought; she might be eighteen.

In my mind, I walk our route in reverse through the enclave. There's nothing to stop me changing my mind. I could walk back, climb the stairs, reach my overseer's hut before Ma Lexie has even gone to bed for the night. She'd have no idea. I could then reconsider, think more clearly, make a sensible decision about my future – I could even plan another escape, when I'm better prepared. I have the key after all. I could go anytime. Why go tonight with Odette?

A short heavy man – looks like a weightlifter – walks one slow step after another along the perimeter wall of the nearest workshop. We wait. He passes by, then heads into the enclave along the next street. My heart is thumping. Would I feel braver a year from now? Yes, much braver, I'm sure of it, and I could make my escape without any help. But Ma Lexie will surely hit me many times before then. Or she'll take away my key – especially when she hears that Odette has escaped. And what if she has an argument with Jaspar? He'd steal me from Ma Lexie to teach her a lesson.

Odette steps out and heads across the open ground. I hesitate and stare at her back as she heads towards darkness. I step out and follow.

We're jogging now, sticking close to the perimeter walls of the workshops. If I felt scared while dodging through the enclave alleys and streets, I feel ten times worse now. Mother and I often walked at night, so I know how dark it can be just a few metres from a lit street. We're lucky there's a three-quarter moon tonight.

Beyond the rough edge to the enclave, Odette takes the solar torch from her bag. "I already checked it," she says. "It works."

"Don't switch it on. Not this close to the enclave," I tell her.

"I'm not stupid."

My fingertips tingle. She's spitting her words at me because she's nervous. It's only nerves. I'm sure. But it dawns on me that I made a mistake five months ago when I first saw Odette. It's possible that I've confused Odette with Gina, back home, who also had dark hair pulled back in a ponytail. At a distance they looked similar. I think Gina liked me, even though she was much smarter. And I liked her because she wasn't a show-off – always looked surprised in class when she gave the right answer. Odette is nothing like Gina.

Leaving the workshops way behind, we cross open ground and reach a deserted road. No headlights in sight. Hardly anyone owns a car in the enclave – not Ma Lexie. I didn't see a car at the family premises; I guess Jaspar doesn't have one either.

It all seems a long time ago – Mother and Father taking me on day trips to the coast. They sold our car to my mother's friend. She came to our flat with the cash, and I went to my bedroom; I couldn't bear to see Mother hand over the keys.

When Father set out on his long journey, Mother insisted he took most of the cash from selling the car. But by the time Mother made up her mind that *we* should leave – the taps had run dry for two months, and bowser water had become way too expensive – we found we couldn't sell anything, none of our furniture or electrical stuff, because so many people had already left. I gave all my games to the few friends who were still around.

Mother spent three days making preparations, packing our backpacks, then unpacking and repacking. I remember the moment she locked the door to our flat. She stood there for two whole minutes, her head against the door, before she withdrew the key from the lock. The queues at the bus station went around the ticket hall three times, and the price of the tickets had doubled since Father left. The bus took us close to the border. That's when we started walking. We couldn't take a bus or a train – we'd be sent back at the first checkpoint.

Men in open trucks were offering lifts, but Mother said, "Don't trust anyone, Caleb! We know where we're headed as long as we stay on our own two feet."

Odette and I stand side by side on the potholed tarmac, facing an overgrown hedge.

She says, "We need to get off the road. There's too much moonlight."

I nod my head. We set off walking along the road. Odette soon picks up the pace. We must have jogged a kilometre when the road veers, and on the bend there's a field gate. We climb onto the middle bar and stare ahead, looking roughly south. I wonder if Odette knows how lucky we are – the field is unploughed. It could be grazing land, but I don't see any cow pats. Without speaking a word, we climb over and that's when I point out the North Star.

Halfway across the field, I call to her. "Odette? Wait. I want to know something." She doesn't stop, or even slow down. I'm four or five paces behind her. "Why did you ask me to run away with you? You could have escaped without me."

She carries on walking, but shouts over her shoulder: "It's safer with two. And it's not safe for me, a girl."

"But what can I –?"

She shouts: "It's just not safe!" She suddenly stops and twists around. "I thought you were older... So *I'll* be looking after *you*. That was *not* the plan."

Without the stars, we'd be lost. We'd be wandering around within the V-shaped land between the two canals. The fields are odd shapes. It would be easy to think we were sticking to a southerly direction when in fact we were heading off in an arc.

We've crossed five fields. The second and third were wheat fields, so we walked the perimeters where the farmers have left strips of grassland a few metres wide – overgrown but still an easier path than crossing the furrows. We climb a stile and find ourselves in yet another wheat field. Odette turns and looks up, checks the North Star again, and says, "I'm tired, Caleb, but we can't stop. We must find the canal tonight."

"Let's hope we don't meet a river. The nearest crossing could be miles away."

Her blank face tells me she doesn't want to hear this.

I reckon we've reached the eighth or ninth field, and the land falls away towards the south into woodland. I have a good feeling. I stride out, take the lead and, all the time, I'm saying to myself that our escape will succeed. It has succeeded! Ma Lexie will be fast asleep now. She won't ever see me again because there's one thing I know for sure – Ma Lexie and the family cannot tell the police I've disappeared; they won't admit they're using illegals. Will they even bother to look for me?

There's a waist-high, barbed-wire fence running along the woods. We throw our bag and backpack across, and I hold the wire down while Odette stretches over. Her trousers snag but she pulls herself free and clambers over, loses her footing and crashes into the ground. She laughs. I laugh with her. It's a relief. She struggles back to her feet and holds down the wire for me.

We wait, our eyes adjusting to the darkness within the woods. I startle as an owl's hoot cuts through the rustling leaves. A more distant owl hoots in reply. Odette is ready to switch on the torch, but we stand still and listen as the owls hoot to one another across the woodland. I hope Odette is thinking the same as me – that the risks we are taking are worth it, right now, at this very moment.

I heard a story once, on the road, of a night just like this when five friends walked through a forest looking, I suppose, for a safe route, wanting to avoid the roads as we do tonight. Although the five friends kept real close, or they thought they kept close, when they reached the end of the forest only four of them walked out. So I decide to walk one pace behind Odette. Not that I'm panicking. I've walked through woods as dark as this before.

She stops and switches off the torch. I step forward to stand side by side with her. She points over to our left. "We're near the edge," she says. "I'm sure of it." She switches the torch on, and we press ahead. And suddenly we're in semi-darkness, the trees thin out and I catch sight of the moon. As we climb up an embankment, I look up towards a star-filled sky. We reach flat ground. In front of us, the still water of a canal.

Which canal, I've no idea. Odette puts her arm around me, squeezes my shoulder. I think she'll be kinder now that she's less worried. "We should rest a while, Caleb, eat a bit of food, then walk along the canal path until first light."

As though we both hold the same fear, that the stars and moon will betray us, we step carefully down the embankment. I sit on my backpack while Odette digs around inside her bag for food. She hands me the torch. "Shine it in the bag." She pulls out two oranges and a bar of chocolate, and she sits down on her bag. I shine the torchlight on her hands as she places the oranges on the ground and snaps the chocolate bar in half. She hands me the chocolate. I see, in bright detail, the thumbnail of her right hand, the half moon of her nail and the seemingly etched lines that run from the half moon to the thumbnail tip.

I see something else.

I take the chocolate, then track her hand with the torchlight. She passes me an orange. It sits in her palm. And I delay a moment in taking it. I squint, looking hard at her fingernails.

"Switch it off," she says. "We don't need the light."

I've seen enough to kill my appetite. The same dark line – it isn't dirt – I've seen my own fingernails in that state after I've stitched a bad wound. A thin line of blood under each nail. I flick the torchlight up towards her neck, see a smear of blood under her left ear.

"Switch it off, will you?" She punches my shoulder.

I don't dare to peel the orange. My hands are shaking too much. I place the orange in my trouser pocket, telling Odette I'll eat it during the walk. I eat the chocolate, but I don't taste a thing.

She asks, "What time will your boss know you're gone?"

"Six-thirty." On Sundays, I tell her, Ma Lexie gets up early for market, but not as early as she does on Saturday. Odette says that we must walk at least ten miles before daylight. Tomorrow night we must walk at least twenty. That way, we should reach Wales and the border country in two or three nights. She must be guessing; she admitted earlier she didn't know the distance. But why quiz her? It's pointless. When we get there, she says, there'll be plenty of work in the vineyards. "We can enjoy the open air and spend all day chatting with the other pickers. I'm totally fed up – having no one to talk to." She picks up the torch and shines it straight into my face. "Why so quiet, Caleb? You can't go back. You know that, don't you?"

"I don't want to go back. I want to go to Wales."

Now that I'm walking along the canal path about twenty paces behind Odette, I replay everything that happened on her roof this evening. Her boss, the old woman, came to the roof with the plate of food. She disappeared from view, and I didn't see her reappear. Next... Odette ran across the roof, and that was when she threw the bottle with the message. Then, Odette came to the edge of her roof and signalled to me: *five minutes.*

I'm in trouble if I stay with Odette. I'm guessing... in a few hours, she'll be wanted for murder. And Odette, I suspect, needs me for cover. The police will be looking for a girl on her own. Not a girl and a boy. In fact, they won't be looking for a boy at all. Because Ma Lexie will keep her mouth shut about me.

The canal surface reminds me of a metal ruler stretching into the distance, silver in the moonlight. I tick off the distance by counting my steps. It's a distraction from thinking about how tired I am. The walk is easy, as walks go, but I'm aching because although I'm stronger than I used to be – thanks to the food at Ma Lexie's – I've lost all the stamina I built up while walking with Mother. You get into a rhythm. You let go of time.

I try to imagine myself with my old friends walking through the countryside close to home. Instead of Odette, I see Leo up ahead. We've slipped out of our homes for a midnight adventure – and we'll return safely to our beds. We pretend we're resistance fighters and special combat troops, working together to blow up bridges. Never in a million years would we pretend we're escaping migrants, with no real plan, no real destination.

In the moonlight, single oak trees stand like sentries positioned across the countryside. In the middle distance, there's a security light by a farm building. The only sounds are our footsteps on the gravel path, the swishing of treetops in the breeze and, just once so far, a dog barking in a farmyard.

I try to keep my thoughts in a straight line. Don't ask Odette any questions. There's no point asking her about the smear on her neck or her fingernails. I can't trust anything she says. Maybe she only wants me along until we're close to Wales, and then she'll give me the slip. If the police find us together, I'll be in as much trouble as her. But *I've* done nothing wrong!

A long line of narrow boats is moored to the bank up ahead. Odette waits for me to catch up, and says, "Walk on the grass edge, slowly. Stay close." We tread past, one deliberate step after another. I'm sure there are people inside. Pots of geraniums have been placed on the roof of one narrow boat. There's an empty bottle of wine in the bow of another. My backpack catches on a long bramble and there's a loud scratching noise as I tug myself free. I stop, look over my shoulder, check I'm clear of the bramble and press on. We stay on the grass until we're well away from the moorings.

The sky is starting to lighten, and the thin mist that hangs over the canal and surrounding fields won't hide us for much longer. I've already heard a tractor. For the past two miles, I've looked for places to hide out. There are gaps in the hedges along the canal path but they all lead into fields. Even if we tried to sleep in a deep furrow, or under the hedgerow, we could be spotted by farm workers.

The path takes us under a brick-built bridge, and Odette says we'll bed down as soon as we find cover. I'm beginning to wish we'd stopped an hour ago. We've passed cottages with long gardens reaching down to the canal side. One had a garden shed, close to the canal. I pointed it out to Odette, said we could break into the shed and sleep there. She shook her head. No discussion. I've also seen a clump of trees in the middle of a field, but I think they've grown around ponds.

About fifteen minutes' walk beyond the road bridge, we come to a good spot where a patch of woodland reaches the path – like the woodland at the start of our canal walk.

"Here," she says. We walk thirty or forty paces off the path until we come across a small dip. She says, "I need a pee. Turn around."

The ground in the dip is damp, so I sit on my backpack. We could sleep on my tarp, but I won't suggest it, because I'll creep back to the canal path as soon as she's asleep and put a few miles between us.

I hear her footsteps – they're quicker than I expect. In my mind, I see her with a rock in her hand. I leap up and twist around.

"What's the matter?"

"An animal. I thought I heard an animal."

She pulls two apples from her bag. "Fruit again."

"That's okay."

"You know, Caleb, finding the canal was the difficult part. We are free."

"And in Wales…?"

"We can join the itinerants, move from farm to farm, pick fruit."

"What happens when all the fruit has been picked?"

She shrugs her shoulders. "We'll work something out. Find an empty house. Grow our own food." Odette pulls on a hat. "I'm tired." She lies down and snuggles around her bag.

Odette's plan is shit.

I move as far as I dare from her and lie down with one arm through the strap of my backpack, like I did when I camped with Mother. What would she think of me now? Mother had a real plan, one with simple goals: reach a reception centre, place our trust in the authorities, work for however long the authorities dictated until we won the right to settle and make a new home. I should never have trusted Skylark. Trusting people like Skylark wasn't part of Mother's plan.

I'm woken by voices on the canal path. Idiot. I fell asleep! Still woozy, I stay still, waiting for the voices to fade. In a flash, it occurs to me: Ma Lexie will have discovered the unlocked steel door. I imagine her running across the roof to my hut, flinging the door open. I hope she feels bad.

I pull myself to my feet. Odette doesn't move at all; she's like a rock. I pick my way as quietly as I can back to the canal and start walking. I check the position of the sun. It's mid-morning. The people I heard on the canal path are now far off, walking north. I stride out, and I'm smiling. I start to jog in case by some sixth sense Odette suddenly wakes. It's better that she thinks I ran away as soon as she fell asleep.

The canal follows a gentle curve and after a few minutes I turn around. Odette wouldn't see me now – the patch of woodland is far behind me. I drop my backpack and take the water bottle from the side pocket. Leaning my head back, I take a swig and feel the two keys move against my chest. I pull the ribbon up and over my head, and I stare at them. Only yesterday the keys marked me out as Ma Lexie's new boy. Holding the knotted end of the ribbon, I swing the keys gently back and forth. With a flick of the wrist, I throw them in the canal.

I'm on my own. It feels good.

I look down at myself. I'd look better in shorts and T-shirt, so I quickly change. Then I jog some more. And as I jog, I decide that I've made some bad decisions since Mother disappeared, but from today I'll stick to the plan. I'll have to find a police station, hand myself in. After all, I have my papers. I can prove who I am, that I'm younger than I look. At least the police will take me to a reception centre, and if I ask nicely they might even look for my

65

parents.

I look over my shoulder again. In the distance, I see a barge heading down the canal in my direction. I stop and watch. As it nears, I see it's loaded with a heap of earth, with an upside-down wheelbarrow chucked on top. A man at the rudder is looking straight ahead, down the length of the barge, as though his thoughts are a million miles away. But as he approaches, I wave and smile. "Nice day, isn't it?" I call out.

He raises his eyebrows, woken from his daydream. He nods at me. The barge passes by, and he twists around.

"Want a lift?"

I shout back, "Not today, thank you."

I can be friendly, but I'm not trusting anyone again. I'll trust my own two feet.

About the Author

Anne Charnock's writing career began in journalism. Her articles appeared in the *Guardian, New Scientist, International Herald Tribune* and *Geographical*. Her debut novel, *A Calculated Life*, was a finalist for the 2013 Philip K. Dick Award and the 2013 Kitschies Golden Tentacle Award for debut novel. Her second novel, *Sleeping Embers of an Ordinary Mind*, was included in the *Guardian*'s "Best Science Fiction and Fantasy Books of 2015."

Learn more about Anne and her work at: www.annecharnock.com www.facebook.com/ACalculatedLife www.pinterest.com/annecharnock and meet Anne on Twitter at @annecharnock

NEWCON PRESS

Publishing quality Science Fiction, Fantasy, Dark Fantasy and Horror for ten years and counting.

Winner of the 2010 'Best Publisher' Award from the European Science Fiction Society.

Anthologies, novels, short story collections, novellas, paperbacks, hardbacks, signed limited editions, e-books...
Why not take a look at some of our other titles?

Featured authors include:

Neil Gaiman, Brian Aldiss, Kelley Armstrong, Peter F. Hamilton, Alastair Reynolds, Stephen Baxter, Christopher Priest, Tanith Lee, Joe Abercrombie, Dan Abnett, Nina Allan, Sarah Ash, Neal Asher, Tony Ballantyne, James Barclay, Chris Beckett, Lauren Beukes, Aliette de Bodard, Chaz Brenchley, Keith Brooke, Eric Brown, Pat Cadigan, Jay Caselberg, Ramsey Campbell, Michael Cobley, Genevieve Cogman, Storm Constantine, Hal Duncan, Jaine Fenn, Paul di Filippo, Jonathan Green, Jon Courtenay Grimwood, Frances Hardinge, Gwyneth Jones, M. John Harrison, Amanda Hemingway, Paul Kane, Leigh Kennedy, Nancy Kress, Kim Lakin-Smith, David Langford, Alison Littlewood, James Lovegrove, Una McCormack, Ian McDonald, Sophia McDougall, Gary McMahon, Ken MacLeod, Ian R MacLeod, Gail Z. Martin, Juliet E. McKenna, John Meaney, Simon Morden, Mark Morris, Anne Nicholls, Stan Nicholls, Marie O'Regan, Philip Palmer, Stephen Palmer, Sarah Pinborough, Gareth L. Powell, Robert Reed, Rod Rees, Andy Remic, Mike Resnick, Mercurio D. Rivera, Adam Roberts, Justina Robson, Lynda E. Rucker, Stephanie Saulter, Gaie Sebold, Robert Shearman, Sarah Singleton, Martin Sketchley, Michael Marshall Smith, Kari Sperring, Brian Stapleford, Charles Stross, Tricia Sullivan, E.J. Swift, David Tallerman, Adrian Tchaikovsky, Steve Rasnic Tem, Lavie Tidhar, Lisa Tuttle, Simon Kurt Unsworth, Ian Watson, Freda Warrington, Liz Williams, Neil Williamson, and many more.

Join our mailing list to get advance notice of new titles and special offers:
www.newconpress.co.uk

NewCon Press Novellas

Anne Charnock – The Enclave

Alastair Reynolds – The Iron Tactician
A brand new stand-alone adventure featuring the author's long-running character Merlin. The derelict hulk of an old swallowship found drifting in space draws Merlin into a situation that proves far more complex than he ever anticipated.
Released December 2016

Simon Morden – At the Speed of Light
A tense drama set in the depths of space; the intelligence guiding a human-built ship discovers he may not be alone, forcing him to contend with decisions he was never designed to face.
Released January 2017

Neil Williamson – The Memoirist
In a future shaped by omnipresent surveillance, why are so many powerful people determined to wipe the last gig by a faded rock star from the annals of history? What are they afraid of?
Released March 2017

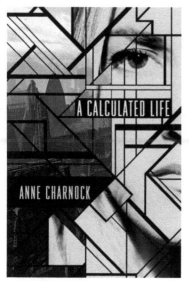

All cover art by Chris Moore.
Also by Anne Charnock:

A Calculated Life

Available now from 47North

"For readers who want a smart, subtle exploration of human emotion and intelligence, this is an excellent choice. Charnock is a subtle worldbuilder, but a convincing one."
– *Strange Horizons*

"Charnock has fascinating, complex things to say about work, sex, family and hope." – *Adam Roberts*

Shortlisted for the Philip K. Dick Award and the Kitschies Golden Tentacle Award.

Coming soon:

Dreams Before the Start of Time

The author's much-anticipated third novel, after *A Calculated Life* and *Sleeping Embers of an Ordinary Mind* (which featured in the Guardian's list of "Best science fiction and fantasy of 2015").

Released April 2017 by 47North

Lightning Source UK Ltd.
Milton Keynes UK
UKHW01f0007220918
329325UK00002B/136/P

9 781910 935347